Ben Elton has proved himself the most popular and the most controversial comedian to emerge in recent years. As well as his own stand-up routines, Ben's numerous writing credits include *Blackadder II, Blackadder the Third, Blackadder goes Forth, The Man From Auntie, The Young Ones*, and the international bestselling novels *Stark* and *Gridlock*. His first play, *Gasping*, was first performed at the Theatre Royal, Haymarket in 1990. *Silly Cow* is his second play.

Silly Cow

A Comedy
by
Ben Elton

WARNER BOOKS

A *Warner* Book

First published in Great Britain in 1993
by Warner Books

Enquiries regarding performance rights to SILLY COW
should be addressed to McIntyre Management Ltd
15 Riversway, Navigation Way, Preston PR2 2YP

A CIP catalogue record for this book is
available from the British Library.

ISBN 0 7515 0190 5

Typeset in Baskerville by 🅰 Tek-Art,
Addiscombe, Croydon, Surrey
Printed and bound in Great Britain by
Richard Clay Ltd, Bungay, Suffolk

Warner Books
A Division of
Little, Brown and Company (UK) Limited
165 Great Dover Street
London SE1 4YA

Silly Cow

Silly Cow was first performed at the Theatre Royal, Haymarket on 20 February 1991. The cast, in order of appearance, was as follows:

SIDNEY	Patrick Barlow
DORIS	Dawn French
PEGGY	Victoria Carling
DOUGLAS	Alan Haywood
EDUARDO	Kevin Allen

Directed by Ben Elton.

Designed by Terry Parsons.

Produced by Philip McIntyre.

ACT ONE

SCENE ONE

It is morning in DORIS WALLIS's *flat.* SIDNEY
sits on the sofa. He likes to think of himself as a
rough diamond. He is a populist tabloid-
newspaper man.

SIDNEY: For Gawd's sake, Doris, pull your finger
out; if you take much longer getting dressed
you'll have gone out of fashion and have to start
all over again.

DORIS *emerges from her boudoir in her expensive,*
gaudy dressing-gown (kimono style), putting
finishing touches to her hair. DORIS *is a big, bold,*
brassy, witty, women's features journalist; she has
her own TV-comment column which is pure
abuse.

DORIS: Sidney, Sidney, Sidney, there may be
cameras. You have to imagine what you're going
to look like in the bitchy photo bit of some
Sunday mag: 'Doris Wallis knew it would be
curtains for her in court, so she decided to wear
a pair . . .' The skirt might take a while, I'm
afraid. Tight little black number, bought in a
spirit of optimism, it's like trying to get a space-
hopper into a gumboot.

(DORIS *retreats into her boudoir*.)

SIDNEY: I must say this business of taking the press to court is becoming rather worrisome. Actresses, novelists, that murderer's Mrs. Where will it end? Is the press to be shackled by an unhealthy obsession with the facts? we ask ourselves. It's going to make for some very dull breakfast reading if everything we write has to be true.

(DORIS *emerges fully dressed*.)

DORIS: Well, what do you think?

SIDNEY: My darling, you look like mutton dressed as a rat.

DORIS: So you've been reading my new Fergie piece then.

SIDNEY: Beautiful bit of work, like watching a mugging. That's why you should be working for me. The stuff is poetry, wasted on your current editor; the clueless arse will probably print it upside down in the sports page.

DORIS: He won't be printing it at all at the moment; I can't copy it through, my modem's down . . . This junk was supposed to make our lives simpler! Let me tell you, I've never had a postman go down on me.

SIDNEY: Well, quite. Tell you what, if you print it up, I'll fax it through for you on the trusty portable.

DORIS: Peggy does my admin, thank you, Sidney.

SIDNEY: Fair enough.

DORIS: I shall put my trust in a simple envelope . . . A couple of days won't matter either way, this piece is timeless. 'Poor fatty Fergie looked like an explosion in a pizza factory. Either the Duchess of Pork has gone psychedelic or young Beatrice had just been sick.'

SIDNEY: Like I said, poetry. You really are a nasty woman, my darling, creeping about making other people's lives a misery. The world lost a great traffic warden the day you opted for features journalism.

DORIS: It's a dirty job but somebody has to do it. I'm the nasty cow who slaughters the sacred cows. Please feel free to have another bucket of Scotch. I'm going to finish my face.

(*She exits.*)

SIDNEY: Doris, darling. Believe it or not I do try and do a bit of work between drinks. Starting a new paper from scratch does require a modicum of time and commitment, especially if you've been away as long as I have. Nobody knows me in the UK any more and I have rather a lot to prove . . . So if you'll just sign this letter of intent then I can . . .

(*We hear her voice from the boudoir.*)

DORIS: Sidney, I haven't time . . . (*We hear her snort loudly.*)

SIDNEY: Call me old-fashioned, Doris, but I could have sworn you were supposed to put the powder on your nose not up it.

(DORIS *re-emerges perkily*.)

DORIS: Looking good is about feeling good, Sidney.

SIDNEY: Yes, well, I'd feel a great deal better with something a little more concrete to show my publishers. Bugger my boots Doris, this is my break! English language editor of the first Euro tabloid! Think of it! Kelvin MacKenzie they could have asked, Derek Jameson, Larry Lamb, anyone, but no, they sent to America for little old nobody Sid!

DORIS: Well, pardon me if I don't chew your trousers off right now and kiss the great man's bum.

SIDNEY: Doris!

DORIS: I've said I'll probably take the job and I really don't see why I should have to sign anything.

SIDNEY: Three months I have courted you, my love, it's three long months since I wrote you from the States! I've got through entire marriages in less time than that.

DORIS: I just have a problem with signing things, that's all. I think I must have been scared by a contract as a small child.

SIDNEY: Don't you trust me?

DORIS: Of course I trust you, Candyfloss. I trust all editors to be dirty, duplicitous little weasels and not one has ever failed me.

SIDNEY: Doris, I have given up everything for this project.

DORIS: You're not the only one who'll be giving things up, Sidney Skinner! You're not the only one who's had to work hard for everything they've got! While you were sneaking around Hollywood trying to buy photos of Jackie Onassis with her fun bags flying, I was dogsbody on the *Preston Clarion*, and I mean dogsbody.

SIDNEY: We all did our time in births and funerals, Doris.

DORIS: Yes, and I'm never going back. These last few years I've finally got a grip of *la dolce vita* and I'm sticking my talons in deep. I am never again going to get up at five-thirty on a rainy morning to report on a sheepdog trial, I am never again going to cover the Liberal candidate in a by-election, and I am never again going to review another show at Preston Rep . . .

SIDNEY: Doris, this is all very interesting but . . .

DORIS: There was this appalling old ham; I'd watched him every three weeks for two and a half years, and whatever part he played, he did his Noel Coward impression. Hamlet's ghost, Noel Coward. *The Crucible*, Noel Coward,

Mother Courage, Noel Coward. Imagine what
the old fart was like when he actually had to
play in a Noel Coward – his accent got so
clipped I swear he was only using the first letter
of each word. So please believe me, Sidney, I am
never going back to that. I've done my time,
Sidney, and now it's paying off. I've got my own
column, I've cooked with Rusty on TV-AM, two
Blankety Blanks last series, and Les called me
Cuddles. What's more, tonight is the big one, I
get my first *Wogan*. These are not things you
throw away lightly, Sidney. Which is why I am
just a little bit hesitant about ending up in
Stuttgart working for an editor I scarcely know.

SIDNEY: Look, you're right to be cautious, Doris,
but this is just a non-binding letter of intent to
impress the krauts. I need something firm.

DORIS: And as far as I'm concerned your krauts
can shove something firm up their collective
lederhosen. I don't like being pushed around
and I certainly wouldn't dream of signing
anything without showing it to Peggy.

SIDNEY: Gawd knows what you think you gain by
showing it to Peggy anyway. You should be
showing it to a lawyer.

DORIS: If Peggy thinks it's necessary, she'll show
it to a lawyer.

SIDNEY: She worries me that one. I can't say as I
like her over much. She's a bit sly, two-faced.

DORIS: Sidney, if Peggy had two faces I doubt

she'd be wearing the sourpuss one she wears at the moment. Anyway I don't want you to like my staff. They're not there for you to like them. Now can you please shut up about Peggy, the letter, and the firmness of your krauts while I get ready for this bloody court case.

SIDNEY: Well, if you really want to know, I reckon that jacket's a bit much for Judge Jeffries.

DORIS: Which just goes to show that you are a tasteless old tart and wouldn't recognize a good thing if it sat on your face and farted up your nose . . . These jugs are worth a character reference from the Archbishop of Canterbury. Not sexy you see, jolly. Anyway it'll have to do, I'm not going to change again. Where the hell are my notes . . . ?

SIDNEY: Well, judging by the way you run your life, I presume Miss Piggy will have them.

DORIS: I don't even know where the bloody court is. If she doesn't get here soon, knockers or no knockers, we shall lose this case by default . . .

SIDNEY: You rely on that girl far too much. She'll get poached by some Channel Four lefty who doesn't think it's a compromise to have a servant as long as he calls her a PA.

DORIS: Lose Peggy? Don't, I wouldn't know where my arse was to wipe it.

SIDNEY: You're a sculptor, Doris, and the English language is your clay.

DORIS: Thank you.

> (*Sound of slamming front door, loud 'so-rry' is heard and* PEGGY *rushes in, brief-case and bag in hand, rather severe brunette hair, efficiently, if slightly dowdily, dressed.*)

PEGGY: Sorry – that latch still isn't catching you know, any manner of nasty type could just walk right in.

SIDNEY: I think one just did.

DORIS: Peggy, where the hell have you been?! This is a bloody important day.

PEGGY: Doris, I don't believe it. The car will be here in half an hour, Douglas is coming around to get the accounts signed, we still haven't got back to that *Wogan* researcher about tonight's show, and you haven't even changed.

> (SID *laughs*.)

DORIS: Peggy, this is my court gear. Just because you choose to dress like you're applying for a mortgage. I am dressed to win. That bitch will take one look at these glad rags and confess to murdering Lord Lucan.

SIDNEY: Of course she will . . . Hello, Peggy.

PEGGY: Good morning, Mr Skinner.

DORIS: Don't call him 'Mister', Peggy, it gives him airs. The man doorsteps queer news-readers for a living.

SIDNEY: We perform a valuable social service, my darling. After all, surely the public has a right to know which of its news-readers are queer!

DORIS: Well, of course it does, Sidney! The right to doorstep queer news-readers is a cornerstone of our precious democracy! Take away that freedom and what have you got? Pravda, that's what!

SIDNEY: Well, quite. Anyway, Peggy, I've been oiling round your beautiful boss for three months now. I think you and I can insult each other on first name terms, eh? Go on, defrost that grimace, call me Sidney.

PEGGY: Yes, but if the deal collapses and Doris decides she doesn't want to be your Euro features editor, that's when I think 'Mr Skinner' would be more business-like.

SIDNEY: Well, you are certainly a cool one, aren't you?

DORIS: Cool? Peggy can freeze a man at twenty paces; I swear sometimes when she opens her mouth a light comes on.

SIDNEY: Well, let me tell you, Doris, if you're thinking of letting her talk you into pulling this deal after I've spent three months with my tongue so far up your backside I know how many fillings you've got . . .

DORIS: Oh, for pity's sake! Look Peggy . . . Sidney wants me to sign this. He says it contains nothing binding.

SIDNEY: Of course it doesn't, it is simply a polite bloody note to a consortium of Huns who are considering paying you mucho marks and loadsa lira to say that you might be interested in becoming their resident Eurobitch. You are not committed, you are not bound, you will not wake up tomorrow to find *The Time Life History of the American Civil War* on your doorstep. All it does is give another little building block with which to assemble the deal.

DORIS: Peggy?

PEGGY: Mr Skinner's right, it's pretty innocuous, but I still wouldn't sign it, Doris. Why should you? If your present boss saw it . . .

SIDNEY: Present boss? What's your present boss got to do with anything? I was under the impression, Doris, that your present boss is about to become your ex-boss.

DORIS: Oh, just give it here . . . Eyebrow pencil do?

SIDNEY: I think not. Blood would be acceptable.

DORIS: Peggy, pen. There, satisfied?

SIDNEY: Satisfied? I don't think I'd go that far. Let us just say that for the time being I have returned the pills and the razor blade to the bathroom cupboard.

(SIDNEY *goes to the sideboard to pour himself a drink.*)

PEGGY: Um, Mr Skinner, Doris and I have business to discuss and her car will be here at twelve to take her to court. I don't want to rush you . . .

SIDNEY: You won't, my darling, you won't. (*Pours himself a drink.*)

DORIS: Twelve, Peggy! But we have to pick up Eduardo!

PEGGY: Eduardo is being picked up first, he'll be in the car.

SIDNEY: Eduardo? Would that be the moody young fellow who was slouching on the sofa, grunting and absent-mindedly readjusting his wedding tackle last time I visited?

DORIS: It would, and so what?

SIDNEY: I really don't think taking him to court is much of an idea, Doris. This toy-boy thing of yours is rather naff. He can't be more than twelve.

DORIS: Eduardo is twenty-one years old and we are very much an item. If he's on my arm coming out of discos but not beside me in my hour of travail, it's going to make me look a bit of a sad old bag, isn't it?

SIDNEY: If you think that the presence of a preening little juvenile delinquent with a courgette in his trousers is going to help your case, you don't know British justice.

DORIS: Sweetheart, you have got your letter.

SIDNEY: Just finishing the old slurp.

DORIS: Well, leave Eduardo out of this.

SIDNEY: All I'm saying is that, if you hear a gentle thud during the judge's summing-up, don't bother to look round – it will be Eduardo's balls dropping.

DORIS: Sidney, do your Teutonic employers want a columnist, or do they want a celebrity columnist?

SIDNEY: Doris, fame is the spur.

DORIS: Right, well, toy-boys are the price you pay for a happening image like mine, so why don't you conserve your stupendous wit for the next waitress you are trying to impress, and let Peggy and me concentrate for one minute on this bloody case.

SIDNEY: Fair enough.

PEGGY: I phoned your brief again this morning and he says it could go either way. People are rather turning against the excesses of the press. Since the Cornwell business there's been Jeffrey Archer and Elton John and any number of . . .

DORIS: Excesses! Give me that. (*she grabs clipping and quotes*) Look, here it is, Sidney: 'What, oh, what makes that silly cow Trudi Hobson think she can act?' and 'Was it a feminist statement to give the part to such a total dog?' . . .

SIDNEY: A robust but acceptable critique.

DORIS: Good-natured, two-fisted, popular copy . . . (*she continues to read*) 'Those huge wobbling, quilted thighs, jammed up against the hem of her hot pants like two great, pink, floppy draught-excluders, made one pray for liposuction on the National Health . . .'

SIDNEY: Fair criticism.

DORIS: Bold, brassy stuff. I just don't see the problem.

PEGGY: I think she was hurt.

DORIS: Hurt! My mother brought up five kids on a widow's pension.

PEGGY: Now, that's not actually true, Doris.

DORIS: Well, somebody's mother did. I cannot imagine what induced the silly cow to take offence!

PEGGY (*with papers*): As you well know, Doris, the centre of her case, apart from disputing the claim that she has concave breasts, and gargantuan love-handles, is the professional slur. You said she couldn't act. She's pushing the detrimental-to-her-employment thing hard, and six months out of work has added to her claim. You must take it seriously.

DORIS: I love it when you're firm with me, Peggy. She's terribly pretty when she's firm, isn't she, Sidney?

PEGGY: Doris, please. The case.

DORIS: I said she couldn't act; Christ, if Roger Moore had been able to act do you think he'd be the star he is today?

PEGGY: Look, you really mustn't be flippant like this in court, Doris; the woman's a wreck, she's lost everything over this case. She was highly respected and you said . . . 'What with the disappearance of the rain-forests, it was ecologically unsound of the Beeb to use such a wooden actress.'

DORIS: But I say that sort of thing about everyone, I am the 'Ratbag of the ratings'. Nothing is sacred – invalids, children; I once single-handedly destroyed a kid's career.

PEGGY: Doris, it's not relevant . . .

DORIS: Absolutely turned him into a national joke. This repulsive, simpering little pre-pubescent tick, looked like a bloody girl. Never stopped working, Dickens' musicals, kid's adventures, became a sort of national pet . . .

PEGGY: Doris, we have to concentrate.

DORIS: I thought, 'Right, my lad, I shall string you up by your first pubic hair'. He did these ravioli ads, grinning away saying, 'I wanta some more, Mama', sucking up great mounds of the stuff, sounded like oral sex in the elephant house. Every week for a month I made a little joke about it. They ended up having to ditch the campaign.

SIDNEY: God knows, Doris, I hope she doesn't win. You've had poison in your pen for half a decade, you could be going to court from now till Domesday. I saw the clippings in America, they're dripping with blood. That bit you did about the New, New Saint, I'm sure his lunchbox would satisfy a starving mouse . . . and the Bleasdale piece saying that bloke's Geordie accent had arrived on Tyneside via Pakistan.

DORIS: Look, I said she couldn't bloody act and she had a couple of whopping great thunder thighs. I'm not a serious critic, everybody knows that, I'm a bitch; my TV page is a column, people read it for the bitching.

PEGGY: The problem is, of course, the woman can actually act a bit – Grotowski, Peter Brook, *Morecambe and Wise Christmas Show*; a season at the RSC.

SIDNEY: Yes, she even came over and did her Juliet and all that bollocks for us in the States.

PEGGY: And you can be certain she'll bring that up today.

DORIS: Oh, and I suppose just because some bunch of over-subsidized, toffee-nosed, bulgie brains happen to appreciate her classical enunciation, our six and half a million readers have to grovel to superior beings, is that it?

PEGGY: I think this is definitely one of your strongest cards. Our lawyer says the judge we've got will love the anti-intellectual bit; if she starts claiming a definitive Desdemona she's in trouble.

SIDNEY: The common touch, that's the way to play it.

DORIS: Of course it is, people actually like my stuff, unlike the almighty RSC which people only pretend to like. We don't need a couple of million a year scrounged off the government to stay afloat.

(*The door buzzer goes.*)

DORIS: Oh, God, that can't be Eduardo yet!

PEGGY: I think it will be Douglas . . .

SIDNEY: And who's Douglas, my dear? Surely not another pouting little three-year-old dago to lend emotional credibility to your case?

(PEGGY *is at the intercom.*)

PEGGY: Hello? . . . Mr Robertson. Please do come on up.

DORIS: Douglas is my accountant, Sidney . . .

SIDNEY: Ah ha, an accountant, eh? A wolf in shit's clothing.

DORIS: He's a decent bloke, Sidney. It'll be a new experience for you.

SIDNEY: And how would you know that he's a decent bloke? He didn't tell you so himself by any chance, did he?

PEGGY: I told her so, Mr Skinner.

SIDNEY: Now, did you really Peggy, so you're a financial expert as well as a legal one, are you?

PEGGY: I took advice from Ms Wallis's bank manager, her agent, her solicitor and independent advisors . . .

SIDNEY: And no doubt came up with some Brylcreemed super yuppy with a portable phone strapped to his dick.

(*A knocking at the door.*)

PEGGY: Just push it, Douglas, the latch is faulty.

(PEGGY *opens the door. Outside is* DOUGLAS ROBERTSON. *He is a dignified old gentleman, leather patches on sleeves, ancient leather brief-case. A kindly, but astute old fellow.*)

DORIS: Enter the yuppy.

PEGGY: Hello, Mr Robertson.

DOUGLAS: Good morning, Peggy, my dear. How very lovely to see you.

DORIS: Hello, Douglas, it's a long way up, you must be knackered; come and sit down.

DOUGLAS: It's thoughtful of you, Doris. Gravity does appear to exert something of a greater pressure on me than in years gone by. Thank you, Peggy. (*she has taken his coat*) I'm sure that Newton missed a trick when he failed to equate increases in gravitational pull with advancing years.

DORIS: He'd have spotted it quick enough if he'd been a woman, Douglas; I'll tell you, without a couple of RSJs under these, (*her bust*), I'd be polishing my shoes with them.

SIDNEY: Nobody puts it like you put it, Doris.

DOUGLAS: I don't believe I've had the pleasure, sir . . .

SIDNEY: Good thing too at your age. (*he laughs a friendly laugh*) Sidney Skinner, Doug, Doris's new boss.

DORIS: Prospective boss, Sidney.

SIDNEY: Have it your own way, precious. Well, here's to the lot of you. (*drains his glass*) Now, then, Doris, I know your diary's about as crowded as the M25, so I'll just take my letter and get out of your short and curlies . . .

PEGGY: Um, Doris, I was wondering if, before Mr Skinner goes, it might not be a good idea to let Mr Robinson take a look at the letter you signed for him. You know, just as a kind of second opinion.

SIDNEY (*hating* PEGGY): Darling, that is mine and Doris's affair and none other's. Besides, as I keep telling you, it's only a letter of intent. It is non bloody binding.

DORIS: In which case, what's the problem?

SIDNEY: There isn't a problem! I just happen to believe in the rights of privacy, that's all.

DORIS: I shall remember that when you ask me to stake out Elton John's bog.

(DORIS *exits to her boudoir*.)

SIDNEY (*pompous*): The lavatories of the famous are news, Doris, it's completely different.

DOUGLAS: Is this letter something you've signed, Doris? You really must be most careful about things which you are called on to sign.

SIDNEY: And what business is it of yours, mate?

DOUGLAS: Excuse me, sir, but Doris's business is my business, I am her accountant.

SIDNEY: Exactly. A bloody ledger filer.

DOUGLAS: It is an honourable profession.

SIDNEY: Honourable profession? What? Convincing the Revenue she spends a grand a week on pencils and Tippex. Listen, Doris, this letter has nothing to do with . . .

DOUGLAS (*quietly very angry*): Neither your letter nor your affairs interest me in the slightest, sir. I am here simply to complete Miss Wallis's accounts.

SIDNEY (*conciliatory*): Well, of course you are. I didn't mean to be personal. I'll tell you what, if you're interested, I've just come back from donkey's years in the States and I've got a fairly substantial but rather dodgy pile hanging around off shore . . .

DOUGLAS: It is quite clear to me the type of accountant that you favour, Mr Skinner. The type who supervised Doris's affairs until she came to me.

(DORIS *re-enters*.)

DORIS: Always have a straight accountant, Sidney. If you've got the dosh you can get away with most things in this country, but one thing Her Majesty won't stand for is not getting her cut. I can't think of anyone better placed to give us an honest opinion on your nasty little non-binding letter than Douglas . . . (*grabs envelope from* SIDNEY) Would you mind, Douglas? (*she hands it to* DOUGLAS) Thank you.

SIDNEY: Yes, by all means take a look, Douglas, and then perhaps Peggy would like to have the bloody thing published in *The Times* so that everybody can get a sneak preview of our plans.

DORIS: Oh don't be such a drama queen, Sidney.

DOUGLAS: Well, as Mr Skinner has so rightly pointed out, I am only an accountant, but even to my lay-man's eyes this document appears to be entirely innocent.

SIDNEY: Thank you.

DOUGLAS: From the brief perusal I have made, it seems to be no more than a vague statement of possible future interest in a Pan-European publishing venture.

(DOUGLAS *returns the envelope to* DORIS's *desk*.)

DORIS: Thank you, Douglas. Better safe than sorry, Sidney.

SIDNEY: Well, you may rest assured that your new and loving boss will be going through your expenses with a nit comb once I've got you in my horrible clutches.

DORIS: Goodbye, Sidney.

SIDNEY: Understood, a nod's as good as a wink. (*Draining his glass he crosses to the table. At* PEGGY) And speaking of expenses, Peggy, let me assure you that personal assistants are not claimable.

(*He snatches up the envelope from the crowded table and makes for the door.*)

PEGGY: Goodbye, Mr Skinner.

(*The buzzer rings again.*)

SIDNEY: Perhaps that's the milkman, perhaps Peggy would like me to show him the letter for a quick once over, just to be sure. After all, his brilliant milkman's eye may spot something sinister that a simple accountant might miss.

PEGGY: Hello? What? But you're miles too early . . . oh, well, you'd better come up. (*she puts down intercom*) It's Eduardo.

SIDNEY: Oh, my Gawd, phone the society for the prevention of cruelty to children. Madam's jail-bait has arrived.

PEGGY: I'm sorry about this, Doris, I distinctly
   told him twelve o'clock.

SIDNEY: He probably needs his nappy changing.

DORIS: Sidney, hilarious though this paedo gag
   is, I consider it a touch rich coming from
   somebody who is going to be regularly exposing
   some poor sixteen-year-old bimbo's bazookas
   Europe-wide simply to provide Joe, Jacques and
   Juan public with the stimulus they require for
   their Euro stiffies.

SIDNEY (*pompous*): The fun-loving photos in my
   newspapers will be there to express a joyful
   appreciation of the fulsome beauty of the
   youthful female form.

DORIS: Sidney, they're there to help people wank.

DOUGLAS (*very embarrassed*): Uhm . . . perhaps
   I've called at an inconvenient time . . .

DORIS: Well, you're here now, so don't worry
   about it.

(*There is a knock at the door,* PEGGY *opens it.*
*EDUARDO stands outside. He is about twenty.
A handsome, cocky, streetwise, male bimbo. He
carries a bunch of flowers.*)

EDUARDO (*walking straight to* DORIS): He's
   here! Hello, beautiful, what's shaking? Wicked
   little number, totally rockin'. I like a bit of
   purple. Wear it for me?

SIDNEY: Honestly, Doris, he'll have to go. See
   you.

(SIDNEY *leaves*.)

DORIS: Eduardo, what the hell are you doing here . . . ?

PEGGY: The car was supposed to pick you up at twelve.

EDUARDO: Came early dinnit. Aren't you pleased to see me? Had me barnet done special. (*checking hair in mirror, he is pleased*) Murder or what? Raving, as it happens. Twenty-three notes, you can't knock it. Here's your good luck flowers . . . Hope you like them, you paid for them.

DORIS: Peggy, do something creative with these, please.

PEGGY: Of course. I'll put them in water, there's some in the lavatory.

(DOUGLAS *clears his throat*.)

DORIS: Oh yes, excuse me, Douglas, this is Eduardo, he's a friend of mine.

DOUGLAS: Good morning, Eduardo.

EDUARDO: Murder, Doug, happening. You one of Doris's toy-boys then? Ha ha ha.

DORIS: Douglas is my accountant, sweetie. Like you, he has to juggle with large and slightly unmanageable figures, but there the resemblance ends. Now then, sugar plum, Douglas and I have a bit of business to go over so you just sit tight and Peggy will make you a little drinkie.

EDUARDO: Awesome. Er, tequila, Peggs. Actually I've got a bit of business for you myself, Doris.

PEGGY: Tequila, Eduardo? You have to be in court in an hour.

EDUARDO: Yeah, gonna be a banging good rave innit? Hope the judge has got a big wig, they're classic them wigs. Tasty or what? I went to court before, chillin' it was, we'd had 'E' so we was wasted, but it wasn't really funny 'cos this Richard I knew got five years. Wish we could have stopped giggling 'cos he was a mate.

PEGGY: Small tequila then?

(*She goes up to fix a drink.*)

DOUGLAS: Five years! Good lord, Eduardo, what had your friend done?

EDUARDO: I told you. He was a Richard.

DORIS: Peggy, Eduardo's drink quite quickly, please.

DOUGLAS: But being called Richard isn't a crime.

EDUARDO: No, the geezer dealt, Doug. He sold gear. Richard, Richard Gere, dealer, you thick or what? He sold . . .

DORIS (*quickly*): I agree with you Douglas, it does seem rather a harsh sentence for impersonating a film star.

EDUARDO: Happening! Here, Dougy boy, have a look at this, eh? (*crosses over and shows*

DOUGLAS *his wrist watch*) Solid gold Rolex. Top watch. Murder innit? Two grand.

DOUGLAS: It looks very . . . uhm . . . reliable.

EDUARDO: I'll tell you what mate, it's reliable bollocks, that's what, ha ha ha. Forty notes. Bangkok, totally rockin'. Have you ever been to Bangkok, Dougy boy? They've got chicks out there who can fire darts out their fou-fous . . .

DORIS: Would you excuse me for a moment, Douglas?

DOUGLAS: Of course, Doris.

(*Rather embarrassed* DOUGLAS *takes papers out of his brief-case and buries himself in his work.* DORIS *beckons* EDUARDO *over, tough and intimidating.*)

DORIS: Eddie?

EDUARDO: What's shakin'?

DORIS: Excuse me. (*pointing at mouth*) This is your mouth. (*pointing at his crotch*) This is your brain. The distance between them is too far for a coherent thought to travel. So if you wish to continue drinking tequila and Hoovering up mirrors at my expense, you will not attempt to bridge the gap.

EDUARDO (*slightly unconvincing bravado*): Keep wishing, girl. You need me because I'm happening.

DORIS: Eduardo, let me tell you an important

fact of life. There are more penniless, loose little
boys in the world than there are rich, single
women. It's a buyers' market, sonny, and you're
for sale. So back in your box.

EDUARDO (*shaken but still attempting bravado*):
Oh yeah, I get you things you need . . . (*he
produces an envelope*) Like, the newspaper
clippings you asked for, you'll love them, they're
fresh . . . (*He speaks this to the room*, PEGGY
and DOUGLAS *are studiously ignoring them.
Then he speaks conspiratorially to* DORIS)
Although some of the lines in them will get
right up your nose, ha ha ha.

(DORIS *grabs envelope.*)

EDUARDO: Now say you don't love me.

DORIS: Eddie, this stuff is just like you. A cheap
thrill, extremely common, and very easily
purchased. Now then, Douglas, what can I do
you for?

DOUGLAS: Well, I'm rather worried about . . .
(*He looks at* EDUARDO.)

DORIS: Oh, you can say your piece in front of
Eduardo, Douglas, he thinks a right-hand
column is something to do with the way your
trousers hang.

DOUGLAS: Well, it's merely your VAT accounts,
they have taken some considerable effort, for
which, sadly, I shall have to invoice you, but I
think I've got them straight. They merely

require your signature and I shall be able to pop them in an envelope and send them to the Custom and Excise people . . .

DORIS: Everybody wants my siggy today. Where do I sign?

DOUGLAS: Well, I'd rather like to take you through them before you sign, Doris. One's financial affairs are not, after all, to be taken lightly.

EDUARDO: Here, Peggy, did you know I can do a Kylie medley in burps?

DORIS: Ed, mouth open, should be shut. Douglas, don't make me try to understand money, I love it too deeply, I love it with a passion, I want to sleep with it and have its babies. How can you ask me to see it as nothing more than columns, numbers and decimal points? Would you have asked Romeo to become Juliet's gynaecologist?

PEGGY: Perhaps if you left them with us, Mr Robertson, Doris can go over them later and then I can get them biked round to you.

DOUGLAS: Posting will be quite sufficient, Peggy. I confess this current vogue for entrusting one's every communication to some leather-clad Apache on a motorcycle leaves me rather cold. I would happily trade a day's delay in my affairs for the comforting sight of an English postman labouring up my path and laying his honest hand on my box.

DORIS: Well, naturally.

DOUGLAS: Since I know that you have a trying day ahead of you, Doris, I shall wish you the very best of luck in court.

DORIS: Thank you and good luck with your postman.

DOUGLAS: Thank you, Peggy . . . and um, goodbye, Eduardo.

EDUARDO (*nearly ignoring him*): Yeah, classic Dougy, banging.

DOUGLAS (*at a loss*): Yes, well . . .

PEGGY (*with him at door*): Thank you, Douglas, we'll be in touch.

(DOUGLAS *leaves.*)

DORIS: All right, Eduardo, go and wait in the car.

EDUARDO: Haven't finished my drink.

(DORIS *crosses to him, grabs drink.*)

DORIS: Bottoms up, my darling. You shouldn't drink so much anyway, it destroys the brain cells, which are not something you can afford to squander lightly. Now, go and wait in the car.

EDUARDO (*sullenly*): Yeah, well I was going anyway, wasn't I. I'm just so wasted. Ravin' night last night.

(*He slouches out.*)

DORIS: Sid's right, that one has to go.

PEGGY: Where on earth did you get him?

DORIS: Oh, he oiled his way up to me in some disco or other a couple of months ago. Luke-warm coffee, Pegs?

PEGGY: No thanks, Doris. I'll stick with my ginseng.

DORIS: Maniac. They all know good old Doris will buy them a few drinks and dust their nostrils. Don't know why I do it really, image I suppose.

PEGGY: It isn't a particularly nice image, Doris.

DORIS: Yes, well, rather more acceptable than my real tastes I think. The honest British housewife appreciates me standing up for womankind, but if she were to discover that I have been known to lie down with womankind, it would be something different altogether. Something, I fear, which would not go down too well with the ironing.

PEGGY: No, I suppose you're probably right.

DORIS: You see, it's different for gay girls. The media does at least have a place for camp, cosy, cuddly old puffs, in their fluffy jumpers. I'm not saying it's easy or pleasant, but there is a sort of niche. I think a cheeky lesbian would be rather more difficult to market, don't you? 'It's just after eight o'clock and time to go over to Doris the dyke with this morning's fashion tips' . . . It wouldn't work you see, the 'top knobs' would object.

PEGGY: I suppose they would.

DORIS: Of course they would. Men as a sex fancy themselves so much they just can't imagine anybody not fancying them.

PEGGY: But really, Doris, Eduardo? It's a pretty unpleasant cover story. I mean rather a high price to pay.

DORIS: Well, I don't sleep with him, do I? You silly cow. Anyway I like having bimbos to push around. People wouldn't think twice if I was a bloke and Eduardo was a dolly bird.

PEGGY: I wasn't prying, Doris . . . I mean obviously I know what you . . . I mean, how you . . . well, the way you . . .

DORIS: Of course you do, Peggy . . . (*casually*) After all, it takes one to know one, doesn't it?

PEGGY: What?

DORIS: Well, doesn't it?

PEGGY: I . . . I don't know what you're talking about.

DORIS: I think you do . . . Anyway, better sign these accounts, get them out of the way.

PEGGY: Aren't you going to check them?

DORIS: What do you think I pay Douglas for? (*She takes up a pen.*)

PEGGY: I'll read them through if you like . . .

DORIS (*having signed*): Too late. You may, at your leisure, bung them in an envelope and bike, post, or spiritually channel them back to dear old Douglas . . . Honestly, Peggy, what a morning! Sid gets worse, doesn't he? I mean, doesn't he? When God was making tosspots he certainly rolled his sleeves up for Sid.

PEGGY: He does grate a bit I suppose.

DORIS: I thank my lucky stars that the chances of me actually having to take his nasty little job in Stuttgart are pretty slim.

PEGGY: I do have to say, Doris, that I can't quite see the need to be so enthusiastic with Sid. If you're really not thinking of taking his job why do you encourage him so much?

DORIS: It's an insurance policy, Peggy, a second option. You never know, my telly plans might fall through, I certainly don't want to end up stuck in my present job.

PEGGY: Oh, but they won't fall through, your ideas are wonderful . . . I finished typing up the treatment yesterday, I left it on the desk there in an envelope.

DORIS: You may think my ideas are wonderful, Peggy. I certainly do, but unfortunately neither of us are commissioning editors at Channel Four and you just can't tell with Channel Four. They keep saying they want to go populist, but somehow they just can't resist those cartoons from Poland. That's why I'm stringing Sid along, just in case the telly falls through.

PEGGY: Not really very ethical, Doris.

DORIS: Please, Peggy, I'm going to cop enough character assassination in court.

PEGGY: Yes, and speaking of which, you really must take it seriously, Doris. The thighs are definitely going to be a problem.

DORIS: Why?

PEGGY: Well the simple facts of the matter are that she couldn't (*refers to notes*) 'tuck them into the top of her socks'.

DORIS: But we went through all this with the lawyer. God knows how many months ago.

PEGGY: Six and a half, I was still temping for the agency.

DORIS: Don't know what I did without you, love . . . As I explained at the time, if these people set themsleves up they should expect to be shot down. The bitch was asking for it.

PEGGY: The question is, does accepting a role in a television drama series constitute asking to be called a silly, talentless, fat old cow.

DORIS: As far as I'm concerned it does. Yes.

PEGGY: I do wish I had your strength of purpose, Doris, I really do.

DORIS: Well, I have a simple philosophy, Peggy, my love. When the dogs are eating the dogs, you have to make damn sure that you're the biggest bitch at the table.

PEGGY: Well, it's all right for you, Doris, but some of us don't find it that easy. Is this your court bag, Doris?

(PEGGY *is bustling about getting* DORIS*'s stuff together*.)

DORIS: Yes.

PEGGY: I'm all right with accounts and business things, I can hide behind a school mistress pose and pretend to be tough dealing with old Sid, but real life's a bit more difficult to cope with. Just coming here today, for instance, there were three men hanging off the scaffolding. I mean it's not as if I'm exactly flaunting it, is it? 'Beautiful arse, love, a smile wouldn't kill you though', two thoughtless seconds for those buggers and I spend the next two hours seething with fury.

DORIS: I'll tell you what you have to do when that happens, Peggy. You must be nice and sweet, never sink to their level. You have to look up, give him a lovely smile, a little wiggle and then you say, (*big sweet smile*) 'Fuck off and die, peanut prick.'

PEGGY: God, you're a hard nut, Doris. I really do admire that.

DORIS: I'm the hardest, Peggy. Bogeymen get scared at night imagining me under their beds. Listen, if people start bullying you, Peggy, you tell me, all right?

(*She pats her hand and holds it.*)

PEGGY: All right, Doris

(*Pause. There is a moment where more might be said between them. But the phone rings.* PEGGY *answers it.*)

PEGGY: Hello, this is the personal assistant to Doris Wallis . . . yes, of course, a car at six, that's right . . . thank you, no, she will be made-up and wearing the clothes in which she intends to appear . . . Thank you, goodbye . . . (*phone down*) That was the *Wogan* people.

DORIS: Oh God, *Wogan*!

(*A distant car horn.*)

PEGGY (*checking watch*): Eduardo's getting impatient. You're all right, Doris, it isn't quite twelve yet. Are you scared?

DORIS: Scared woman, don't be absurd. (*putting on coat*) I shall return without a stain on my character or my underwear.

PEGGY: Aren't you just a little bit sorry for this silly woman? I am a bit.

DORIS: Good. Good, because it's when other people are feeling sorry that I'm at my happiest, Peggy. I have to be, I'm a journalist, I have to be pleased when other people are sad.

PEGGY (*nervous laugh*): You do enjoy cynicism, don't you, Doris?

DORIS: I'm not being remotely cynical, I'm stating the obvious. I remember exactly the first time I realized the truth about my job . . . There was a bomb you see, unexploded, and I knew I wanted it to go off.

PEGGY: Oh, Doris, you didn't.

DORIS: Of course I did. All of us poor runny-nosed hacks did. We'd stood waiting for hours. If it didn't go off, what would we have to show for a day's work? Nothing. Then it did go off and we were pleased.

PEGGY: Yes, but you weren't actually pleased.

DORIS: Peggy, I was delighted. It was a particularly good bomb too. It killed a little boy and a little girl . . .

PEGGY (*upset*): Doris, please, you don't mean that!

DORIS: Peggy, if nobody dies, the article's on page six. I'm on page six. What do you want me to tell you? That I hope I never come across a decent story? That I hope I never get a page one by-line?

PEGGY: Well, no, news is news, it isn't wrong to want to report it . . .

DORIS: And what happens when you stop reporting news and start looking for it? For instance, you've got your sports hero, the new footballer; my editor wants some news: 'Does he screw around? Does he beat his wife?' . . . So I dig and I dig and it turns out the man is a decent bloke. What's my reaction? It's the same as the bomb, Peggy, I'm angry, I'm frustrated, I swear I am sat at my desk wishing that a man beat his wife!! That isn't very nice, is it, Peggy?

PEGGY: Well, no but . . .

DORIS: No, it isn't. I know how tough I have to be to do my job. I know I certainly do not require hysterical self-indulgent actresses getting a judge to run it in. (*putting on scarf*) I'll see you when I see you.

PEGGY (*emotional*): Good luck, Doris. I'll be with you all the way.

(*Lights down*).

SCENE TWO

After a couple of seconds the lights come up again. DORIS *puts her bag back down again and takes off her coat. It is late afternoon. She has returned from court elated.*

DORIS: The prisoner has returned!!

PEGGY: Doris!

DORIS: Champagne, Peggy, bugger *Wogan*, I'll do it a bit sloshed. I want to get so full of fizz, if I uncross my legs I'll shoot out of the window.

PEGGY (*anxious*): So you pulled it off? You got away with it?

DORIS: 'Pulled it off! Got away with it!!' I wasn't flogging a dodgy car, woman! I was defending my honour and professional integrity. I didn't 'get away' with anything. I wittily, elegantly, and with great restraint shat on her and rubbed her face in it.

PEGGY: So I take it you won then?

DORIS: Not quite actually won, no, but as good as. They upheld her claim, but get this, Judgie said he was sick of these big libel awards and that, personally, he thought that saying a girl had gargantuan love-handles was a compliment and advised the jury accordingly. She got a tenner damages and no costs.

PEGGY: No costs! She'll be completely bankrupt, ruined.

DORIS (*mock serious*): I know, Peggy, and I'm devastated, perhaps you'd better phone the Samaritans before it all becomes too much for me.

(PEGGY *gets the champagne*.)

PEGGY: All right, all right, I was only remarking.

DORIS: A symptom of your celebrated weakness, Peggy, you must toughen up.

PEGGY: All right, tell me every little mouth-watering detail.

DORIS: Mouthwatering is exactly the word, Peggy, this case was the legal equivalent of an Opal Fruit. Wait for it, you are simply not going to believe this. They actually measured the silly cow's saddle bags in court.

PEGGY: No!

DORIS: Some old bailiff, you know the type, face like a gas bill, had to scurry off for a tape measure . . . He came back all solemn with a little bag from Woolworth's, 'Ninety-two centimetres in trousers, m'lord', he says . . . I have never seen a woman look a more complete turd in my entire life. I'll tell you what, she's earned her tenner.

PEGGY: It must have been excrutiating.

DORIS: We cringed . . . All except the judge, that is, he's getting all frisky and chipping in that either way a fellow likes something to grab hold of. It was comedy mayhem, believe me.

PEGGY: Ninety-two centimetres had better not be big; I must be about that or more . . .

DORIS: Of course it isn't big, which I suppose is one of the reasons why the silly cow won her case. But the reason she's got nothing out of it is because she's a stupid self-righteous shit and we could all see it. I said it, I said to the judge, I said, 'Come off it, Judgie! . . .'

PEGGY: You didn't!

DORIS: Well, something like that. I said, 'It's bloody obvious that Trudi Hobson is a beautiful woman; she is pert, gorgeous and chewable, with ravishing blonde hair and a lovely figure . . .' I said, 'If a woman like that can't take a good-natured slagging, Gawd help us poor

dogs who live in the real world. There are
people out there dying of cancer for God's sake!'

PEGGY: You don't live in the real world, Doris . . .

DORIS (*enjoying her champagne, drains glass,
refills it): Minor point. People think I do.
Anyway the judge was lapping it up, wasn't he?
Not often for him he gets a dock full of sauce
buckets debating the size of their fondle fins.
Lucky for me he was a jolly old goat, he was
leering away from the start with his wet, watery,
yellow eyes, shining like a couple of raw eggs.

PEGGY: Was she playing up to him?

DORIS: Was she hell. She was glaring at the floor,
I've seen more moving performances in a
Renault ad; but I was giving it full cleavage,
nothing too obvious, you know, (*she thrust out
her chest*) just that look I've got that says 'wrap
these round your ears, mate, and I'll breath on
your bald patch'.

PEGGY: Didn't the prosecution say anything?

DORIS: What could they say? 'Objection, m'lud,
but will you kindly stop leering at the defendant's
coconuts.' There are certain things you just
don't tell a judge, Peggy. Anyway, then we got
into the bit about acting. God you would have
loved it . . . She said she had brought the case
on behalf of all those in the public eye who were
at the mercy of a new breed of gutter journalism.

PEGGY: Sounds a bit righteous.

DORIS: Made me want to carpet the court. I said, 'Judgie, this is nothing more than special pleading from a typically self-obsessed actress. So I said she couldn't do her job? There are kids out there taking heroin and nobody gives a damn!!'

PEGGY: And was this argument judged admissable?

DORIS: Well, not really, the judge told me to stick to the point but he was nice about it. Luckily for me this woman was her own worst enemy. She called me a brute and a bully. Can you believe it, a bully! It was like something out of a *Girl's Own* annual. A bully. I just said I was entitled to my opinion and that she simply could not act. I was sorry but she was a wooden, lifeless performer with all the genuine histrionic talent of a weatherman and it was my duty to express that fact to the public.

PEGGY: And what did she say?

DORIS: She cried, the bitch. I could see the judge going gooey, so I said that crying, m'Lord, is one of the best performances she would ever give; the court loved it.

PEGGY: Did anyone mention the RSC?

DORIS: Of course they did, and that was when I clinched it. I mean honestly, Peggy, apart, of course, from the RSC, who gives a toss about the RSC? Ninety per cent of the population never visit the theatre. Nine per cent of the remaining ten have a nice Aberdeen Angus and then go and see *The Milkman's got my trousers*,

and who goes to the RSC? Eight rows of ponces
on the mailing list and fifteen hundred
extremely pissed-off school kids.

PEGGY: I don't know if that argument's really
fair, Doris.

DORIS: Of course it's fair. Anyway, the court
must have thought it was fair because, as I say,
she won technically but lost in reality, and I, my
faithful friend, am off the hook.

PEGGY: Well, congratulations, Doris, thank God
it's over.

DORIS: Over for me, I don't think it will ever be
over for her. I truly believe she's gone
completely mad. After we left the courtroom she
sort of flipped. She ran up to me and, quite
frankly, I've never seen such hatred in anyone.
She started to scream at me.

PEGGY: What did she say?

DORIS: She said . . . Oh, it's too bloody stupid,
let's forget it.

(*Evening is falling, the curtains are still open,
and very slowly, it is getting darker.*)

PEGGY: What did she say, Doris?

DORIS (*quietly*): She said I was going to die.

PEGGY (*concerned*): Not really?

DORIS: Yes, really. Die publicly. Scorned and
humiliated, just as she had done.

PEGGY: I knew this woman wouldn't be stopped by a judge. She needs help.

DORIS (*suddenly screaming*): 'Viper! Slut! Filthy cockroach!!!'

PEGGY (*shocked*): Please, Doris.

DORIS: That's what she called me. Right outside the courtroom. Her make-up was all tear-streaked and caked, and she was wearing plenty of it. I have never seen a woman with so much make-up on; she looked like a witch with psoriasis. She threw herself down in front of me and started to tear at her clothes.

PEGGY: What? In front of everyone?

(PEGGY *has hardly finished her question when* DORIS *hurls herself down before her, grabbing at her.*)

DORIS (*screaming again*): 'Yes, yes, you're going to die! I swear I'll make you die. You have no human heart, you cannot feel, your soul is the soul of a witch. It is rotten, cold and dead and you must die! You're poison, do you hear me?! Bitter, bitter gall!' And then she turned and ran for a taxi, as if the hounds of hell were after her.

PEGGY: Poor woman.

DORIS: Yes, I must confess I felt a twinge. (*slightly thoughtful pause . . .* DORIS *snaps out of it*) Still, sod her, eh? We won! (*Drains glass*) And tonight we celebrate.'

(*Black out.*)

ACT TWO

Act Two begins at the exact point that Act One left off. The lights come up to find DORIS *raising her empty glass.*

DORIS: Champagne and pizza, that's what we need! Plenty of time before the *Wogan* car comes. Champagne and pizza is the food of the gods and I'm going to stuff it, I'm going to shove it, I'm going to smear pizza all over my body, till I can do an impression of a car crash . . . (*grabs phone and dials*) . . . What do you want on yours, Pegs? I'm having the lot . . .

PEGGY: Oh, just a vegetarian please, no peppers, no chilli, no capsicum.

DORIS: A vegetarian, no peppers, no chilli, no capsicum! . . . (*someone has answered the phone*) Hello? Look, I'm afraid I'm going to have to call you back. I appear to be ordering for Mahatma Gandhi. (*phone down*) Peggy, this is a celebration, you cannot order a dry pizza base.

PEGGY: I'm not, I want cheese and tomato, it's called a Neapolitan.

DORIS: A pizza, Peggy, by any other name would

be as crap. Calling it a 'Neapolitan' means nothing, you could call Little and Large the 'Neapolitan' Brothers and they'd still be two Mogadons in velvet bow-ties. This is a party and Neapolitans are not invited.

PEGGY: All right, I'll have a few mushrooms.

DORIS: Then let the orgy begin. (*she dials again*) This is the start of a whole new time for me, Peggy, I can feel it. I've dealt with that jumped-up actress, I've got more career options than an ex-cabinet minister, I'm about to order a pizza! I'm in Heaven.

PEGGY: Beware hubris, Doris.

DORIS: What's that, something peppery? All right, I'll tell them to hold the hubris.

PEGGY: It's Greek.

DORIS: Oh, I love all that stuff, chick-pea, fish roe . . .

PEGGY: It's an ancient Greek term. It means pride comes before a fall.

DORIS: Well, who's a Mrs Hoity Toity . . . (*into phone*) No, not you, I've just got a classically educated kill-joy ordering at this end. All right, got your pen ready? I'd like one (*jokingly scornful*) 'Neapolitan', please, with three and a half mushrooms, and two, very large, very deep whoppers, with everything on, yes, that's right everything you've got, the tables, the chairs, the phones, extra hubris. If there is a restaurant cat, slaughter it, put the meat on one and the pelt on the other. Cheesecake, fudge cake, and garlic bread twice. Good, that's the penthouse flat, Morley Mansions. And could you send a slightly less hormonally imbalanced adolescent this time. The last lad who came, I nearly tipped the pizza and ate his face . . . Ta, gorgeous. (*phone down*) Now then, Peggy, let's have another glass of that fizz. I feel fantastic.

PEGGY: It really is good to see you so happy, Doris. You didn't say anything but I knew you were worried about that case.

DORIS: Well, the woman was so determined, I thought she might sway the judge by just being a mad old witch. That scene outside the court proves she's a lunatic. Yes, there's no question, I'm glad it's over and I can concentrate on the future.

(PEGGY *brings more champagne*.)

PEGGY: Yes, let's drink to the future.

DORIS: Up yours, Peggy. It looks pretty bright to me. I'm on a roll, Peggy, everything is opening up for me, and what's more I want you to be a part of it.

PEGGY: Well, I want to be a part of it, Doris, you know that, but it's not easy.

DORIS: Now don't be stupid. We've become a team, you and I. Whether I stay in London or go to Stuttgart, you've got to be there.

PEGGY: Oh, you won't be going to Stuttgart, silly, you know Sid's horrible job is a last option. You'll get the telly.

DORIS: Well, stranger things have happened.

PEGGY: I must say I'm a bit concerned about that letter he made you sign though. Supposing you let Sid down and then lost the telly, you'd have to stay where you are. That letter would be a nasty little document to end up on your current editor's desk.

DORIS (*happily slightly tiddly*): Peggy, please, I want you to imagine that this small bunch of grapes is our friend Sidney's testicles. (*She snips off the grapes*) Now, were that man to do the dirty on me, I swear, Peggy, I should have his scrotum wrapped round my carriage return and . . . (*she has dropped the grapes into the machine . . . she types the keys very hard*) write his epitaph on them! (*She finishes and viciously slams the carriage return.*)

PEGGY (*reprovingly*): Well, you're planning to do the dirty on him, Doris.

DORIS: I am an artist, Peggy, can I help it if I'm being extensively courted?

PEGGY: You're being extensively deceitful.

DORIS: That's my prerogative, I'm the one with the talent, let me tell you, Pegs! Once I get a proper shot at telly, all the European Currency Units in Germany wouldn't get me back to print.

PEGGY: I'm sure they'll take your idea, it's so wonderful, so many shows in one – a talent show, a magazine, a chat show, a weekly review. The title's brilliant.

DORIS (*standing exuberantly with her glass*): 'A view from the Bitch'.

PEGGY: I did laugh while I was typing it, when I wasn't trying to decipher your shorthand. Did you really mean Eurovision 'Pong' Contest?

DORIS: I most certainly did. It's a Demean the Public section. Guess a bloke's nationality by smelling his breath.

PEGGY: Oh, I see.

DORIS (*rummaging on table*): So where is this bloody treatment then? I want to make sure you got the Mugging section right.

PEGGY: Well, it made sense to me. Basically it seems to be a question of taking a handbag from a woman in the audience and showing everybody else what's in it.

DORIS: You'll never be a poet, Peggy . . . Oh, look, can you believe it? (*finds envelope*) Sidney didn't take his letter after all, drunken old fool.

PEGGY: I'm sure he did, I saw him take it.

DORIS: Well he must have put it back, honeyplum, because it's still here and so we remain gloriously uncommitted.

PEGGY (*concerned, looking over table*): Doris, the

treatment I typed for you was in an envelope like that . . .

DORIS (*worried*): What? You mean it looked like this? (*Holding up* SIDNEY's *letter*.)

PEGGY: I . . . I think so . . . (*realizing*) Oh, my God.

DORIS: So we've got Sid's letter and he's got my treatment. (*urgent*). Get Sid on the phone . . . (PEGGY *is halfway to the phone when the doorbell rings*. PEGGY *and* DORIS *look at each other* . . .)

DORIS: It can't be the pizzas, it'll take a month to cook what I ordered . . .

(PEGGY *crosses to the intercom and answers it*.)

PEGGY: Hello? . . . Oh, hello, Mr Skinner . . . Yes, come on up.

DORIS: Shit.

PEGGY: He sounded all right.

DORIS: If he's taken a look in that envelope there's no way he's going to be all right.

PEGGY: What if he just sent it straight off? I mean, what will the Germans make of it?

DORIS: Oh, we'll get away with that, I can't see them making much out of the Eurovision Pong Contest. But if he's read it . . . Oh, well, we shall see, Peggy.

(*A knock at the door*. PEGGY *opens it*, SIDNEY *is outside*.)

SIDNEY (*cheerfully*): Hello, Peggy.

PEGGY: Hello, Mr Skinner.

SIDNEY: Doris, darling, you won't believe it but your old pal must have had a brain transplant with a house brick. After all that bloody fuss over the letter . . .

DORIS: I know, you forgot it. (*She has it in her hand.*)

SIDNEY: Gawd, am I thicker than an elephant's sandwich or what? (*he takes it from her*) Thank my stars, thought I might have lost it. (SIDNEY *takes the paper up stage and, with his back to the audience, puts his brief-case on the sideboard or something. He opens case as if to put paper in; there seems to be a bit of faffing around.*)

SIDNEY (*cheerily*): Well now, Doris, you old jail-bird you, tell old Sidney how you got on in court today. I didn't see anything on the news.

DORIS (*still not knowing how to play it*): Rather well actually. I won basically. Although the silly cow went completely mad afterwards and threatened me with death outside the court.

SIDNEY: Blimey, that's a bit upsetting, I must say.

DORIS: Oh, don't worry about it, she's harmless enough. All actresses are completely bonkers, they have lobotomies and electric baths at drama school. Ha ha ha!

SIDNEY: No, I mean it's a shame about you

winning your case. I don't deny that seeing you dragged off to Holloway in chains would give me greater satisfaction than touching up the gusset on a blurred telephoto shot of Princess Stephanie's crotch.

DORIS: I beg your pardon.

SIDNEY: You, Doris, are a lying, two-faced slag.

DORIS: So you read the treatment then?

SIDNEY: Yes, I read it. Congratulations, it was very very good. Rather a complex show to pull off whilst holding a full-time job in Stuttgart, of course, but nonetheless, very, very good.

DORIS: Thank you.

(*An embarrassed pause.*)

PEGGY (*nervously*): Um, drink, Mr Skinner?

SIDNEY (*without looking at her*): Fuck off, Peggy.

DORIS: Um, I'd rather you didn't address my friends like that.

SIDNEY: Oh, friend is it? I thought she was just some downtrodden little wage slave . . . (*to* PEGGY) I hope you realize, Peggy, that you're probably next under Doris's dancing duvet. Has she started suggesting you wear something prettier yet? Something pink and lacy. Take care, my little virgin prune, this nasty old slut will be under your hem like a greased whippet.

DORIS (*suppressing great anger*): And just what is all that supposed to mean, Sidney?

SIDNEY: Come off it, darling one. It's a bit stomach-turning watching a wicked old devil like you trying to play the innocent. Everybody knows about your little preferences, don't they? Except that sad bit of juvenile rough trade, Eduardo, you drag around . . . He knows now though, I rung him. Cor, those Latin types can't half swear.

DORIS: Bit pathetic wasn't it, Sidney? Telling tales to some dirty, stoned kid . . .

SIDNEY: I'm going to make you regret your lack of standards, Doris.

DORIS: Oh, for God's sake, all right, I've been investigating other work. So what? It probably won't come off, and then you and I will be spitting blood at each other in Stuttgart as if nothing had happened.

SIDNEY: I'm not going to Stuttgart. I've already faxed them, I've blown it out.

DORIS: Sidney, you're raving. You reckon that because I've been a bit of a naughty girl, you're going to make yourself redundant?

SIDNEY: I'm not going to be redundant, darling. At least I hope not. If negotiations that I put in train this afternoon come off, I'm going to be fronting an outrageous new talent, magazine, chat show on Sky TV.

DORIS (*very heavy*): What are you talking about, Sidney?

SIDNEY: Oh, I know it seems unlikely, dear. An old tart like me becoming a star, but I have got a certain common touch, don't you think? And anyway, the ideas I had to offer, well, the producer had a bloody orgasm. I must say, I thought he'd be pleased, ideas were rather good you see . . . the 'Pong' contest, the handbag bit, great for a man to do it too.

(DORIS *starts forward*. SIDNEY *grabs a bottle*.)

SIDNEY: Don't you bloody hit me, you gorilla-faced dyke!

DORIS: I'll sue you for plagiarism . . . !!

SIDNEY: Oh, yeah? Who have you got? You and your mousy little girlfriend here? Don't make me damp my jocks. I'll get a witness too, I'll get ten. Copyright is about proving first ownership, my gorgeous old sauce. My idea's with a producer at Sky, who's seen yours?

DORIS: Sid, you pig, if you pull this off, which you won't let me tell you, I shall crucify you every week in print for ever. What I did to that silly cow in court today will look like a character reference from Postman Pat.

SIDNEY: Not in your present rag it won't, my dear. You see, as I believe I mentioned earlier, this case has a portable fax machine in it, Cellnet you see, very clever. (*he takes the letter of intent out again*) I didn't think that your current editor would take kindly to you signing a letter of intent to German publishers, so I've sent him a copy.

DORIS: You . . . didn't!

SIDNEY: I did, my love. Faxed it through to him just now. If the lazy sod's still at work he'll have it by now . . . (*walks to door*) So there you go, Doris, Europe's out, you've almost certainly lost your present job, and I've nicked your game show. That is what you get for being a dirty double-crosser. (*He exits. DORIS rushes to door and shouts after him.*)

DORIS: You're dead, do you hear me, Sid, Dead!

PEGGY: I'm so sorry, Doris . . .

DORIS: I can't believe it, the bastard, I've got to think . . . Why did you make me drink that bloody champagne, Peggy? I've got to think . . . I need something to help me think . . .

(*She crosses to sideboard. She is looking for something. She searches for a moment.*)

DORIS: Peggy, I've told you never to clear anything up, or throw anything away from here.

PEGGY: I haven't . . . What . . . ?

DORIS: An envelope that Eduardo brought round . . . There was an envelope here when I left for court!!

PEGGY: An empty envelope, yes . . .

DORIS: It wasn't bloody empty! It had a little package in the bottom of it, an important little package.

PEGGY: A package of what?

DORIS: Never mind what, where's the bloody envelope?

PEGGY: I . . . I . . . used it.

DORIS: Peggy, what do you mean?

PEGGY: I always re-use old envelopes . . . I've got these resealing stickers from Friends of the Earth . . . It was empty, I . . .

DORIS (*shouting*): It wasn't bloody empty!!

PEGGY (*very upset*): Please, Doris, don't shout, I don't understand. What was in it?

DORIS: Never mind what was in it, who did you send it to?

PEGGY: It was your VAT tax forms from Douglas.

DORIS (*exploding in disbelief*): The Customs and Excise!! You sent eight grams of cocaine to Her Majesty's Customs and Excise!!

PEGGY: Cocaine? Doris, I had no idea you . . .

DORIS: Where's my passport? I've got to pack! Peggy, phone the travel agent, I have to get out. Oh, my God! I've got to pack. This can't be happening!

PEGGY: I didn't send it to Customs, I sent it to Douglas.

DORIS: Douglas?

PEGGY: That was what I was supposed to do, wasn't it?

DORIS (*stopping*): Douglas? That's better . . .
probably wouldn't even know what it was, don't
think he'd shop me . . . Peggy, get him on the
phone . . . (PEGGY *grabs phone*) . . . Look at
these, Peggy . . . (DORIS *goes to her desk, she starts
grabbing handfuls of envelopes*) Envelopes,
envelopes, we are surrounded by hundreds of
bloody envelopes . . . Peggy, the trees are
already dead, I don't think they would have
minded . . . Oh, God, why me!

(SIDNEY *appears at door again, with* EDUARDO.)

SIDNEY: Knock, knock. Excuse I. Just wait and
see who I've found, trying to kick the door
down; he's bust your outside lock . . . Thought
I'd bring him up, wouldn't want to miss the fun.

(*He leans arrogantly against the door as*
EDUARDO *pushes past him.*)

PEGGY (*to* DORIS): Douglas is out. (*puts phone
down, crosses to door*) Eduardo, this isn't a good
time.

(EDUARDO *is furious – seething with injured
pride. He looks ready for violence.*)

EDUARDO: Oh, yeah, Pegs doll? I reckon it's a
raving good time. Awesome. Anybody want a
couple of lines of Gonzales? It's top gear,
banging good stuff. 'Columbian'. Got it off a
Rasta. Totally wasted my box. Murder, man.

DORIS: Get out, Eduardo. I'll phone you.

EDUARDO: You can stick your phone up your
brown-eyed cyclops, you horrible old tart.

DORIS: What?

EDUARDO (*shouts*): Why didn't you tell me you was a muff muncher?

DORIS: Listen, sonny, I'll tell you exactly what I like and when I like, and what I'm telling you now is to fuck off and take your foul, fucking mouth with you.

EDUARDO (*beginning to let his anger show*): Listen, Babes, I don't mind being pampered but I ain't being used, all right? I got standards. I'll take 'em fat, I'll take 'em ugly, but I don't take them queer. You made a fool of me. You . . . you made me look dirty in front of the geezers.

DORIS: Excuse me, but this is now becoming just a touch comical. I've had a tabloid editor talking about privacy, now I've got a rather inexpensive toy-boy saying he feels soiled. Well, you are soiled, Eduardo, that's how you were born. Brillo pads and liquid gumption couldn't raise the ghost of a shine on you.

(EDUARDO *leaps forward and grabs her*.)

EDUARDO: Yeah, and you're a dirty pervert! Your sort should get put away! Bloody corrupt kids you do!

PEGGY: You leave her alone you . . . peanut prick!

(EDUARDO *turns on* PEGGY.)

EDUARDO: What's shakin' now, eh? What'scooking, Pegs? Raving got you, ain't I? Raving got you, you old dog.

(*He raises his fist to strike*.)

PEGGY: Hit a woman would you, you coward!

EDUARDO: Why not? I ain't Saint raving George, am I? Besides, your kind ain't women. Bet you molest kids, it's always in the papers that stuff is. Makes me want to have a right classic spew.

DORIS: Peggy, phone the police, tell them we have two dangerous intruders . . .

(EDUARDO *calms quickly*.)

EDUARDO: No need for all that.

SIDNEY: Oh, don't trouble yourself on my behalf, I shall be off shortly. Just finishing my drink and watching the fun . . .

DORIS: All right, Peggy.

EDUARDO (*triumphant*): You want to know something, Doris! You thought you kept your little secret pretty good, didn't yah? Well, I've blown it, yeah, classic giggle. Stitched you up proper, you slag. Want to know what I did? I told the papers. Awesome, eh? I told them about us and what you really are . . .

SIDNEY: 'Teenage toy-boy denounces middle-aged celebrity girlfriend as gay'.

DORIS: I am not middle-aged!

(EDUARDO *goes to door*.)

EDUARDO: So see you, doll, gonna have a decent
  rage for once, ain't I? Do some blow, get on
  some 'E'. Hang out with some happening
  people, people who ain't half dead. You won't
  see me again. Except one thing, babe, we'll be
  together one more time, in the Sunday papers,
  ha ha ha! Awesome, eh?

SIDNEY: Thank you for the drink, Doris . . .
  Actually, you won't believe this, but I'm sorry.
  You're having a slightly more rotten evening
  than even I had planned.

DORIS: You've got five seconds.

SIDNEY: OK. Just trying to be nice.

  (SIDNEY *pauses for a second, then exits. Long
  pause.*)

PEGGY (*pretty shaken*): What . . . what are we
  going to do, Doris?

DORIS: Something very strange is going on,
  Peggy, too much is happening at once.

  (DOUGLAS *appears at the door. He is stern and
  angry. He is holding the envelope.*)

DOUGLAS: The outside door-lock has been
  forced, I presume by those two hooligans I just
  passed on the stairs. Anyway, I took the liberty
  of coming up.

  (PEGGY *and* DORIS *jump.*)

DORIS: Hello, Douglas.

DOUGLAS (*sternly*): Good evening, Miss Wallis.

DORIS (*nervously correcting him*): Doris, Douglas.

DOUGLAS: I think under the circumstances I would prefer a less familiar form of greeting.

DORIS: Circumstances, Douglas?

DOUGLAS: I was with the Customs and Excise for fifteen years, I know the hellish stuff when I see it.

DORIS: Well, don't cry about it for God's sake. It's only for private, recreational . . .

DOUGLAS: Oh, private is it? Damn strange kind of privacy, popping it in with your VAT returns and sending it to your accountant. It's the breathless arrogance of your kind that makes me so very angry. Why do you consider yourself so different, Miss Wallis? Why is it that people like you, fashionable people, can indulge yourselves in any kind of unhealthy, anti-social activity that you choose and continue to lead comfortable, respectable lives, while half the civilized world watches its children die over stuff like this . . . (*He shakes the envelope at her.*)

DORIS: Look, Douglas, I'm having a particularly tough day today and I'm not sure I'm up to a moral debate.

DOUGLAS: No! No, I don't think you are up to a moral debate, you nasty, hypocritical woman.

DORIS: Douglas, I'm sorry the stuff has offended

you so much, I really am, and I'll think about what you've said . . . but, for now, why don't you give it me back and then you can forget all about it, eh?

DOUGLAS (*very angry*): Do you know there are Asian women doing fifteen years in Holloway for getting this stuff to you? Poor, clueless mules. I know, I caught a few, and a bloody depressing business it was too. Fishing small, damp packages out of people's bottoms made me feel like a bloody magician.

DORIS: Yes, well I'm very sorry for them . . .

DOUGLAS: Good! Good! I'm glad you're sorry for them, it's nice that you're sorry for them, because you're shortly going to have the pleasure of being able to tell them so yourself.

PEGGY (*stunned*): Douglas, no!

DORIS: What the hell are you talking about, Douglas?

DOUGLAS: Oh, come now, Miss Wallis, you know me well enough to realize that I am not and never have been one of these types, so common in the last decade, who believe that they need only obey those parts of the law which they choose. Oh, well, I know you think me a senile old fool.

DORIS: Yes.

DOUGLAS: It doesn't matter anyway, I just

wanted you to understand my point of view. It's a police matter now.

(*He turns to go to the door.*)

DORIS: You'd better stop right there, Douglas! (*Grabs paper-knife.*)

(DOUGLAS *is at the door.*)

DOUGLAS: How very fitting, how very apt. My entire thesis is confirmed, out comes the flick-knife, the switch-blade.

DORIS: Douglas, it's a paper-knife.

DOUGLAS: Rich or poor, this is where drugs will inevitably lead you. It will be gang colours, automatic assault rifles and shoulder-held missile launchers next. Goodbye, Miss Wallis. I am sorry for you.

DORIS: Grab him, Peggy.

(DORIS *drops the knife, leaps at him and grabs him. But* DOUGLAS *spins her round and pins her to the wall.*)

DOUGLAS: Don't be a fool, madam! I was eight years a soldier . . .

DORIS: Peggy!!!!

(PEGGY, *who has discreetly been getting something out of her handbag, leaps forward and coshes* DOUGLAS, *who falls to the ground senseless . . .*)

PEGGY: Oh, my God!

DORIS: Oh, my God. (*approvingly*) Nice move, Peggy. I had no idea you carried a cosh. (*She grabs envelope, checks it.*)

PEGGY: My mother makes me.

DORIS: And quite right too. Thank you very much, Douglas and, incidently, when you wake up you're sacked.

PEGGY (*kneeling beside* DOUGLAS, *stunned*): He's dead.

DORIS: He can't be.

PEGGY (*very upset*): He is.

DORIS: The bastard.

PEGGY (*suddenly she screams hysterically*): Ahhhhh! What have I done, what have I done? I've killed him! Why didn't you tell me you took drugs, why didn't you say?

DORIS: Come on, Peggy! Calm down, love, calm down. We're in this together, we'll work it out. (*hugging her*) We've got plenty of time, we'll make a plan. Yes, that's it, we'll make a plan. Nobody knows about this, nobody's coming to get you . . . Nobody's coming to get you.

(*The doorbell rings. They both jump mightily. Both scream.*)

PEGGY: Save me, Doris, you've got to save me, I don't want to go to prison . . .

DORIS: Nobody's going to prison, stay calm, stay

calm. (*crossing to the bell, gingerly answers it*)
Hello . . . (*to* PEGGY) It's the pizzas. (*into
intercom*) I love you but we don't really want
them anymore, we . . . Oh, all right, the front
door's broken, come on up. (*to* PEGGY) Can
you believe it, he wants his money . . .

PEGGY: But . . . but . . . if he comes in here he'll
see . . .

DORIS: Don't be stupid, he's not coming in here,
is he? You've got to calm down, take this money
and meet him at the stairs and pay him . . .

PEGGY: Well . . . No, I can't.

DORIS: You've got to, everything must be as
normal as possible. Now we're going to get
through this together, Peggy. So take some
money, go outside and pay the pizza man . . .
and don't mention the corpse.

PEGGY: Right.

(PEGGY *reluctantly takes her handbag and goes
out.* DORIS *takes the envelope and hides the
drugs carefully. Suddenly all the lights go out.*
DORIS *screams in shock in the darkness. She
lights a lighter and finds her way across to the
sideboard which has a couple of candelabras.
She begins to light them.* PEGGY *appears at the
door, laden with pizzas.*)

DORIS (*peering*): Is that you, Peggy?

PEGGY (*shaky voice*): Yes, it's me . . . the lights
have gone out.

DORIS: I know that, Peggy.

PEGGY: It must be a main fuse, the whole building seems to have gone, the emergency lights are on in the stairwell.

DORIS: Well, it's nice to know that some misfortunes are not exclusive to me.

(*She has all the candles going, the light is dim and flickering.*)

PEGGY (*laden with enormous pizza boxes*): I've got the pizzas.

DORIS: I'm not really hungry anymore. We have to do something with this body.

PEGGY (*weeping on her shoulder*): How . . . there's people in the street, on the stairs, we'll be caught, I know we'll be caught.

DORIS: Well, if we can't get it out, we've got to give it a good reason to be here . . .

PEGGY (*trying to think*): Well . . . well . . . he came to check something about your accounts.

DORIS: Yes, not bad as far as it goes, but it doesn't explain why he's dead, does it?

PEGGY: It's my fault, Doris, I killed him, I should take the consequences. What . . . what if I cosh you as well, to prove you weren't involved, then call the police and tell them I went mad?

DORIS: I don't know if you noticed, Peggy, but the last time you coshed someone they ended up dead.

PEGGY: Well, I could be gentle.

DORIS: No, I don't want you to.

PEGGY: Well, what if I tied you up?

DORIS: Yes, good thinking, Peggy, not bad, but it's got to look like he was the aggressor. Yes, that's good actually, Peg. Now come on, tie me up, we'll do it here.

PEGGY: Have you got any rope?

DORIS: Yes, loads in the bedroom.

PEGGY: Good. Why?

DORIS: Never mind about that now . . . I'm scared of fires, it's for escaping, now go and get it. It's in the wardrobe, Peggy, and there's a set of handcuffs under the pillow, bring those as well.

PEGGY: Right.

DORIS: Now, we've got to get the plot straight. These are the basics, Peggy, OK? We plant the coke on his corpse so that we can say he came round to blackmail me, and in the process ties me up.

PEGGY: But, Doris none of these things happened.

DORIS: I know that, Peggy, but he's not here to deny it, is he? Now tie me up!

(PEGGY *reluctantly begins to do it*.)

PEGGY: I still don't see . . .

DORIS: God, you're so thick sometimes, Peggy. Listen, he's tied me up, right? He's threatening me with blackmail, OK? You return, having popped out for some hubris to put on the pizzas . . . there's a struggle, during which you triumph, all right? It's just our word, there's nobody else to tell a different story, we'll get away with it. Tighter, Peggy, it has to be convincing.

PEGGY (*struggling*): I'm doing my best, Doris . . .

DORIS: Ow! Yes, that's tight enough, I can't move.

PEGGY: There, that's pretty good, I was a Girl Guide, you know.

DORIS: Fascinating; handcuffs. Now get the coke from under the typewriter, I hid it there. Put it in his pocket and then you can ring the police . . .

(PEGGY *gets the envelope. Returns to* DORIS.)

PEGGY: I'm scared, Doris.

DORIS (*gently*): Don't be scared, Peggy, I'll look after you. Really, Peggy, I mean it. I'll always protect you. Now just put the package in Douglas's pocket . . . (PEGGY *puts it in* DORIS*'s pocket*) No, Douglas's pocket, Peggy, watch my lips, darling. Put the drugs in Douglas's pocket . . . (PEGGY *is still tightening*) Put the drugs in Douglas's pocket.

PEGGY (*gently, but straight into* DORIS*'s face*): So,
   I can't act, can I?

DORIS: What?

PEGGY: So you don't think I can act.

   (DORIS *screams suddenly. In the flickering
   half-light* PEGGY *tears off her brunette wig;
   underneath she is blonde.*)

PEGGY (*shouting in* DORIS*'s face*): Viper! Slut!
   Filthy cockroach!!! You have no human heart,
   you cannot feel, your soul is the soul of a witch.
   It is rotten, cold and dead and you must die!
   You're poison, do you hear me?! Bitter, bitter
   gall!

   (PEGGY *is Trudi Hobson; she now becomes her,
   turning before our eyes into an eccentrically
   mannered actress. Her walk changes into the
   slightly showy elegance of those who value their
   dance training, no matter how many years ago it
   was. Her accent becomes the casual but terribly
   refined drawl of those who have been taught how
   to speak properly. She pushes her wild blonde
   hair off her forehead. The quiet, mousy* PEGGY
   *has completely vanished. Although she will
   continue to be called that.*)

PEGGY: Yes, darling. It's me. The silly cow you
   said couldn't act. Well, I've acted pretty well the
   last six months, haven't I, darling? (*walking to
   the door*) I'll just make us more cosy, shall I?
   Wouldn't want to be disturbed, would we? Now,

I can pop the fusette back in so you can take a really good look at who I am.

(*She steps outside for a moment . . . The lights come back on.*)

DORIS: This isn't possible.

PEGGY: That's theatre, love. The art of the not-possible, a wonderful world of make-believe which we, the actors, make you believe in. Oh, it's easier than you think when one puts one's mind to it. A good cossie and wig, impeccable references forged by a sweet, sweet prop master I know. I offered maximum enthusiasm for minimum salary and you fell for it.

DORIS: But it's . . . it's so totally out of proportion.

PEGGY: Out of proportion? Darling, you ain't seen nothing yet. The play isn't over.

DORIS: What are you going to do?

PEGGY: Destroy you, my dear. I swore from the very first moment, win or lose, I would bring you down. Oh, it hasn't been so very arduous. Seven hours acting, three days a week. At Rose Bru' we thought nothing of improvising through the night; all we needed was a bottle of cheap plonk, a fragment of Strindberg and we were in Heaven.

DORIS: You're mad, totally raving barking out of your ruddy tree!

PEGGY (*pouring herself a drink*): Well, do you

know, I think all actors have to be a little mad,
or how could we do what we do? We're so very
different from ordinary people, you see. We
hurt so very deeply. That is why I had to plan
my wicked plan, do you see? I had to do it. The
actress in me said I must. And, oh, what a
performance! The most wonderful and fulfilling
of my career.

DORIS: There is a dead accountant on the carpet!

PEGGY: Yes, that's a bonus I must say.

DORIS: Peggy . . .

PEGGY: Trudi, darling. Peggy is a character, a
part; I loathe these young actors who can't
distance themselves from their characters, don't
you? It's so silly.

DORIS: Trudi . . .

PEGGY: All that method rubbish about 'becoming'
someone, well it's just Americanized bollocks,
darling, it really is, absolute Yank wank. An
actor acts, for heaven's sake, it's a job of work
and a bloody hard one too.

DORIS: Six months, Trudi, six months you've
kept up this bit of 'acting'.

PEGGY: Well, you paid me, and, besides, I was
resting anyway. Oh, there was a bit of telly
around, but nothing happening in the West End
at all. The place is a morgue.

DORIS: Six months, I mean, why for God's sake?

PEGGY: Oh, I know it was naughty and I shouldn't have done it, darling; we in the business are always taught to develop a thick skin where the reviews are concerned . . . How, I ask? It's absurd – ask an actor to develop a thick skin? You might as well ask a flower to develop iron petals . . .

DORIS: But it was just a comment, Trudi, a bit of news print . . .

PEGGY: It damn well hurt. I mean, obviously one knows that all reviews except the sweet ones are maddeningly silly drivel, the ravings of a lunatic, and what's more, a lunatic who simply has not taken the trouble to understand the piece . . . but you are not even a critic, you wicked woman, you and your kind are no more than mindless bullies. Can't act!! Can't act, by God! I've destroyed your life by acting. I've acted you to the ground. It was I who switched papers on that repulsive man Skinner so that he took away your equally repulsive show treatment . . .

DORIS: Yes, all right, very clever but . . .

PEGGY: It was I who informed him of your queenly sexuality, in the hope that he might use it against you.

DORIS (*getting angry*): Listen, you mad bitch . . . !

PEGGY: It was I who quite deliberately used your envelope full of drugs to send off your accounts.

DORIS: It was you who killed a man, Trudi! He's

lying there in front of the sofa and forgive me
but I don't notice him applauding your
performance.

PEGGY: I didn't kill him.

DORIS: Yes, you did, you coshed the silly old git
and he died.

PEGGY: Oh, don't be absurd. What would Trudi
Hobson the actress be doing in the flat of her
arch enemy, murdering people? I've never been
here, I don't even know where it is . . .

DORIS: Now come on, Peggy . . .

PEGGY: Exactly, Peggy! Who's Peggy? A shadow,
a figment, nothing more than a performance.
Without me she's gone. And I won't be here. So
perhaps it was you that killed Douglas . . .

DORIS: I didn't kill him and you know it. Peggy
killed him.

PEGGY: I say again, who's Peggy? She's fading
fast . . . Did I play her? It seems so strange, after
all (*into* DORIS's *face*) I can't act, can I?

DORIS: Listen, Trudi Hobson, you are obviously
deeply and irredeemably mad, but please, for
me, make an effort, clutch for a final moment at
the coat tails of Mrs Sanity as she scuttles from
your mind forever, and understand that I will
not be taking your rap.

PEGGY: But, my dear, I really don't see how you
can avoid it. Because when the police get

involved, as eventually they must, there will only be you and the corpse left on my little stage.

DORIS: Whenever the police get involved I'll still be tied up, or perhaps he tied me up after he got killed?

(PEGGY *begins to collect her things*.)

PEGGY: You won't be tied up, I wasn't that good a Girl Guide. You'll worm yourself free eventually, you'll have to. Your answerphone is on and Peggy's last act was to cancel your appointments. You'll either untie yourself or starve. And when you are free again, you'll be all alone with the corpse and the cocaine and it will be your turn to create a convincing performance.

DORIS: Sid, Eduardo, they know Peggy existed. They'll say Peggy was real.

(PEGGY *is putting the wig back on – preparing to depart*.)

PEGGY: I really can't see either of those two low-life's getting involved in a murder enquiry on your behalf. And as to the others I've dealt with, I've been careful to do your business strictly by phone. There are very few people who have caught so much as a glimpse of shy, retiring Peggy. Still, you can ring them when you get yourself free, if you can find your phone book, which I doubt, after all, as you've often said in the last month or two, without Peggy you wouldn't know where your arse was to wipe it.

Which, since Peggy is a figment of my imagination, doesn't say much for you, you nasty, pig-ignorant bully.

(SIDNEY *appears at the door.*)

SIDNEY: Someone mention my name?

DORIS (*enormous relief*): Sidney, thank God you're here.

(SIDNEY *hovers at the door.*)

SIDNEY: Well, it's very nice of you to say so, Doris, I had no idea we were still friends. Just come back for my fax machine – always forgetting it.

DORIS: No, Sid, look she's tied me up.

(SIDNEY *advances into the room.*)

SIDNEY: Well, there seems to be something of an orgy going on here.

DORIS: Sid, you don't understand.

SIDNEY: Oh, I think I do, Doris – don't mind me, I'm broad minded, I've travelled. No chance of a 'ménage' I suppose?

DORIS: Sidney, listen to me. Peggy's not Peggy . . . She's that actress, she's killed Douglas. Look, he's dead.

(SIDNEY *sees the corpse which had been shielded from him by the sofa.*)

SIDNEY: Bugger my bollocks!

PEGGY: She's gone mad, Mr Skinner. She killed Mr Robertson. I had to tie her up to restrain her. Now, I'm just going for the police, so will you please let me pass?

DORIS: Don't let her go, Sydney. Look at her hair, it's a wig.

(SIDNEY *peers at* PEGGY.)

PEGGY: Don't you dare touch me, Mr Skinner. Don't you dare.

(*He reaches out and plucks off her wig.*)

SIDNEY: It's Trudi bloody Hobson.

PEGGY: Yes, it's Trudi bloody Hobson. I fooled you just as I fooled that literary pigmy over there. Even though, apparently, I can't act.

DORIS: Oh, shut your face, you stupid mad cow. Sidney, you've got to restrain that woman, she's gone totally berserk.

SIDNEY: Why should I?

DORIS: What do you mean, why? So we can phone the police and have her locked up in the looney bin for criminally insane actors . . .

PEGGY: Please, don't send me to the National!

DORIS: What are you hanging around for, Sidney. Tie her up or something.

SIDNEY: No.

DORIS: What?

SIDNEY: I'm not going to help you.

DORIS: Sidney, please.

SIDNEY: I'm going to let Peggy's little plan take
    its predetermined course, as if I'd never come
    back for my fax machine. (*gives* PEGGY *back
    her wig*) No point messing with a good script, is
    there? Can't go changing the ending just
    because some old arse like me blunders in from
    the wings. No, on the whole I think I shall leave
    you two witches dancing around your cauldron.

DORIS (*desperate*): Sidney, please help me.
    You've got to help me!

SIDNEY: I'm afraid old Sid the pig can't help you,
    my saucy darling . . . After all, who's Sidney?

DORIS: What?

SIDNEY (*walking up to her and straight in her face*):
    So I can't act, can I?

DORIS: Oh, my fucking God.

(SIDNEY *now drops his sid yobbo character. He is
an actor, a tough, northern one, Liverpool
Everyman or Glasgow Citizen type of thing, strong
regional accent. Plenty of leftish, earthy posing, but
every bit the 'actor' that* PEGGY *is.*)

SIDNEY: I was bloody superb in that Alan
    Bleasdale series, but obviously a Tory cow like
    you working for a Tory rag was never ever
    remotely going to even try to understand the
    piece. That wasn't genuine criticism, that was
    political propaganda.

(DORIS *tries to speak. But is too gobsmacked*.)

PEGGY: You were, Tom, you were quite superb.

SIDNEY: Of course I was. When I played that Bleasdale brickie on BBC2, I suffered more than any real brickie has ever suffered, I worked harder than any brickie has ever worked! I was every brickie.

PEGGY: So in many ways you worked as hard and suffered as much as all the brickies in the world put together.

SIDNEY: Well, I think that's what Alan wanted.

PEGGY: Marvellous text.

SIDNEY (*turning back to* DORIS): So there's me taking the collective suffering of the entire building trade on my shoulders, without claiming my full equity tea-break entitlement I might add.

PEGGY: God, you're a trooper.

SIDNEY: And what did you have to say? I got my flipping accent wrong!! You stupid cow!!! His accent was supposed to be wrong! That was the whole point, the poor bastard didn't know who he was! That was what I was trying to say, I mean I really wouldn't have minded if you'd taken the trouble to understand the piece.

DORIS (*still a bit stunned*): So you've been working with each other from the start.

PEGGY: It's my production, I sought Tom out . . .

You were marvellous darling, truly
incandescent.

SIDNEY: Aye, well it's worked out bloody well,
hasn't it? (*kicks corpse*) The death was a bonus
though, that'll really stitch the cow.

PEGGY: Well, exactly. But you really were
marvellous.

SIDNEY: No, no, you were, much tougher role.
I could just go for laughs, you had to carry the
emotion, the content.

DORIS: And so what's next for the Bonkers Twins
then? Two ends of a pantomime Napoleon in
Looney Bin, the Musical?

PEGGY: My dear woman, as I have explained, we
are actors, we are supposed to be a little mad.
And now, sadly, it is goodbye, Miss Wallis, I do
hope you enjoyed our performance.

DORIS: No.

SIDNEY: I was on that building site for an entire
morning – I knew those men.

(*They are leaving.*)

DORIS: Stop, please. Come back.

PEGGY: Well, darling.

SIDNEY: I suppose we must.

(*They walk back into the room.*)

DORIS: Good. Right, let's just talk about this as
adults, what is it you want from me . . . money?

(*They bow.*)

DORIS: (*calling out*): What! What are you doing? You can't do this to me!!

(*They bow again . . .*)

SIDNEY (*to* PEGGY): One more, love?

PEGGY: No, I think we'd be milking it. Drinky time I think.

(*They leave. There is a long pause.*)

DORIS: (*struggling*): Come back!! Come back, you mad actors . . . (*she struggles again*) Come back . . . (*more struggling, dramatically she screams at the top of her voice*) All right, I admit it, you can act, you can act, you can act!!! . . .

(DOUGLAS *raises his head from the floor and speaks in a huge actor's voice.*)

DOUGLAS: Act. And what about me, you horrid woman!

(DORIS *shrieks.* DOUGLAS *leaps up. He is now not* DOUGLAS *at all, but an actor of the old school, a deep velvet-voiced lovey, who never got to play Lear, a mad, outrageous old ham.*)

DOUGLAS (*huge voice*): 'Blow winds and crack your cheeks!' . . . (*tiny voice*) 'Tell me not now that Little Nell is dead' . . . (*he walks over and stands over her*) Isn't that acting, madam! Have I not the muse!!!

DORIS: I want my mum.

DOUGLAS (*a huge performance*): Just so have I, a thousand times, yearned for the comfort of a mother's breast, when I recall your cruel jibe, 'Dickhead of the Day'. Twice in the *Preston Clarion* did you give me such a title! 'Ham' you called me! Ham! I, madam, am an actor!!! I know of no such meat. Noel Coward impressions, I knew the master quite well actually and he would have laughed at the suggestion.

DORIS: So you're not dead then?

DOUGLAS: No, foul woman, I am not dead. I live to taste the sweet knowledge that you thought I was dead, just as you thought I was your accountant, whom Peggy so conveniently found for you. You thought both these things, foul lady, even though, apparently, (*into her face*) I cannot act . . .

(EDUARDO *appears at the door*.)

EDUARDO: Happening, what's shakin' slag.

DORIS: Oh, Christ.

EDUARDO (*walks in*): Thought this geezer was your accountant, now he's tying you up. (*to* DOUGLAS) You giving her a portion or what? (*to* DORIS) He your toy-Grandad then? Happening. Anyway, if you two are up for a bit of rumpy-pumpy, I won't keep you, just wanted some dosh for that toot I scored you, I forgot before . . .

DORIS: Come off it, Eduardo, get it over with, pull your nose off and show me who you are . . . Felicity Kendal?

EDUARDO: Oh, this is classic, what have you been puffing, Doris? I wish I'd had some, it must be banging good gear, eh, Dougy boy?

DOUGLAS: I answer to no such name, young man.

EDUARDO: Eh? You been blowing and all have you?

DORIS: Eduardo, don't tell me you're a real person, you're not an actor!

(EDUARDO *glares at* DORIS. *Suddenly he drops the wide-boy act and becomes what he is, a beautiful, sensitive, pretentious, young actor.*)

EDUARDO: Actors are real people, you bitch. Just because we're talented and special doesn't mean we don't bleed. People still call me 'that poof off the ravioli ads', because of you. I was making fifty thousand pounds a year when they dropped me. I had to give up my clowning, my mime classes. I am a half-trained mime! Can you imagine the emptiness? I know how to get into the glass box but I can't get out of it.

DOUGLAS: Poor boy. How you young lions torment yourselves.

EDUARDO: Yes, thanks mate.

DORIS: This isn't happening.

(PEGGY *and* SIDNEY *re-enter*.)

PEGGY: I see that you two loves have both had your *coup de thèâtre*'s then?

DOUGLAS: And sweet it was, my dear lady, sweet it was.

EDUARDO (*anguished*): I wasn't happy with mine, it was a disaster . . . It wasn't centred, it wasn't consistent . . .

DOUGLAS: But, my boy, you were wonderful, wonderful.

EDUARDO: No I wasn't. I was crap. I know I was crap, oh, God, I don't know why I even kid myself that I can act. It's a joke, a ruddy joke, me an actor?

PEGGY: Oh, darling!

EDUARDO: Ha! I know I'm better than any other actor of my generation, but what the hell does that prove?

DOUGLAS: Poor, dear boy, tearing yourself apart inside. You'll learn, young fellow, you'll learn. Suffering is part of your apprenticeship . . . (*to* SIDNEY) I enjoyed you, Tom, that was a wicked improvisation though, kicking me while I was down – I nearly grunted.

SIDNEY: Oh, I knew you were too much the pro for that, mate.

DOUGLAS: Ah, yes, playing a corpse is a tough job of acting. So many young fellows think you just have to be physically still. Wrong! You have to be brain dead.

SIDNEY: Anyway, pays you back for putting that tampon in the handbag when we were doing *The Importance* at Hull, do you remember?

DOUGLAS (*laughing*): God, that's a good story, that one. The tampon in the handbag in Hull. I don't think Trudi's heard that one.

PEGGY: Do you know, I don't believe I have.

DORIS: Oh, God!

SIDNEY: Well me and this hell-raising old sod were playing *The Importance* at Hull, freezing cold winter, no heating in the dressing rooms. And then one night his nibs here decides to raise a little Hades. Well, my liege only goes and puts a tampon in the handbag, doesn't he!

(PEGGY *shrieks*.)

DOUGLAS: God, we raised some hell though, didn't we?

SIDNEY: Aye, we supped some decent pints.

PEGGY: A tampon, priceless.

EDUARDO: When I'm on stage, I'm dying inside.

SIDNEY: And so you should be at your age. You can raise some hell when you've learnt your flipping craft and not before. If you're looking for an easy life in the theatre, become a bloody agent.

PEGGY: Oh, don't, mine's a nightmare – ten per cent for bugger all.

(*They are all about to tell their agent stories.*)

DORIS: Excuse me, I don't want to keep you, I know you're all anxious to get your strait-jackets fitted but do you mind if I clear up one or two points here?

PEGGY: Of course, an actor must always encourage audience feedback.

EDUARDO (*squatting down*): Perhaps we should workshop it?

DOUGLAS: I fear you must count me out if you do, dear boy. I would look an absolute sight in a leotard.

DORIS: I just want to get the plot straight . . . There never was a Euro job?

PEGGY: Of course not.

DORIS: And nobody has stolen my idea for Sky, or told the press about my girlfriends, or faxed Sidney's letter to my boss?

SIDNEY: Props love, ever heard of 'em? The actor is given an empty case, the audience perceive a portable fax machine. That is what makes actors special.

DOUGLAS: Here, here.

EDUARDO: Hey, Tom. I think it would have been really good if you'd mimed the case. What do you think, mate?

SIDNEY: Somehow I don't think she would have bought that, son.

DORIS (*cutting in*): And no one's told the police about my little habits, or anything . . .

PEGGY: Nothing has happened, darling, nothing at all. It was a play, don't you see, you've just been in a play.

SIDNEY: And now the play is nearly over.

DOUGLAS: Drinky time.

PEGGY: Here, here.

EDUARDO: I might join you if there's time, but I like to unwind, alone, for a moment or two after the catharsis.

SIDNEY: Well, yes, a couple of years carrying a spear in laddered tights will knock that out of you, son. But now our audience must applaud us . . . (*Gestures at* DORIS.)

(PEGGY, DOUGLAS and EDUARDO *exit.*)

DORIS: What?

SIDNEY: Oh, yes, the most important part is yet to come. You, Doris Wallis, and you alone, must applaud us all. We must hear your ringing approbation, your heartfelt tribute to actors who, in your humble, ignorant opinion, can act . . . Can you do it?

DORIS: (*woodenly*) Yes.

SIDNEY: Go on, have a little practice, we don't want to spoil the final moment . . .

(DORIS *claps*.)

SIDNEY: Oh, come on, I think we deserve more than that. (DORIS *claps louder*) Right, keep it going . . . And so ladies and . . . well, lady anyway, it's a small audience, but it's not the size of your audience, it's the size of your performance. So would you, Doris Wallis, please welcome back into your sitting room Quentin Hopkins who played the part of Eduardo the toy-boy . . .

(EDUARDO *enters and takes a bow as* DORIS *applauds,* DORIS's *chair is upstage, so the bowing is back to the audience.*)

SIDNEY: I think one or two 'bravos' might be in order, eh?

DORIS (*woodenly*): Bravo.

SIDNEY: All right, son, don't milk it. Kelvin Cruikshank as Douglas Robertson the accountant . . .

(DOUGLAS *enters and bows,* DORIS *claps and bravos.*)

SIDNEY: And myself, Tom Warwick, Sid the editor . . . (*he bows and raises a fist*) fight the cuts.

DORIS: Bravo, (*pause*) you wanker.

SIDNEY: And finally, you will be applauding our leading lady, who for the remainder of the evening will be taking over the part of Doris Wallis!!

(PEGGY *enters. She is dressed exactly as* DORIS, *her hair and make up are the same, she looks just like her.* DORIS *stops clapping.*)

DORIS: What?

SIDNEY: Oh, yes, she said you were going to die, Doris, die the public humiliation that she did. And you will, pal, you will . . . tonight your public will watch you die.

(*The bell rings . . .* EDUARDO *answers it . . .*)

EDUARDO: Hello . . . (to PEGGY) It's the car for *Wogan.*

PEGGY: Tell them I'll be right down.

(*Blackout. The end.*)